TOWER

DANIEL ARTHUR SMITH

Tower

Copyright © 2015 Daniel Arthur Smith

ISBN-13: 978-0692572801
ISBN-10: 0692572805

Edited By
Crystal Watanabe

Cover By
Daniel Arthur Smith

Also Written by Daniel Arthur Smith

The Cameron Kincaid Adventures
The Cathari Treasure
The Somali Deception

Literary Fiction
The Potter's Daughter
Opening Day: A Short Story

Horror Fiction
Agroland

Science Fiction
Hugh Howey Lives

~*~

For Susan, Tristan, & Oliver, as all things are.
&
To my cousin Nate who served my country as a Ranger
and now serves as a Citizen.

~*~

~1~

Nate planned this day, this entrance, visualized it, plotted it. The escalator to the right would take him directly from the underground PATH station to his new job without him ever having to step outside. But he wanted to go to the street. At least today. He wanted to see the building he'd be working in for himself — One World Trade. He cranked his neck back so he could take in the magnificent tower from base to spire. He was awestruck, as he imagined he'd be. The September sky reflected off the hundred and four floors of glass, steel, and... freedom. He'd come full circle in a way. Circle-like. He wasn't a New Yorker. He was from Florida. But every step he'd taken over the last fourteen years had to do with the piece of land where he stood. He'd set out on a journey that took him halfway around the world, only to end up right back at the site of the catalyst — Ground Zero.

Nate had other ideas of what he was going to do when he returned. Jobs were scarce and what civilian training did he have? He'd spent his entire career in special operations, supporting tier one missions in both Iraq and Afghanistan, four deployments in all. Sure, he could've gotten a job with NYPD or the government, but neither paid well.

That was okay though.

Titan had called him looking for a few good men. Men like him.

He inspected the plaza, the fence to the memorial, the angle of the tower glass, and the cloud reflecting in it. He nodded his head and straightened the jacket he'd picked up at Men's Wearhouse the day before.

A foot in the door was all he needed. This was day one. This was New York. If he could make it here...

~*~

~2~

When the lights went out, Nate figured New York was being hit.

He hunkered down.

He hunkered down the same way he had all those nights in the dark stony hills of Afghanistan. His first day on the job, the first day at Titan, and WHAM!

He hadn't even finished filling out the stack of paperwork the woman from HR had given him.

Nate heard the whimpers in the blackness — a lot of them — confused pleas for help, the crying.

He heard the screams — on his floor, the floors above, below.

Nate was calm.

This was not the first time he'd heard these sounds, the cries of the helpless.

There'd been many firsts in his life since the building that stood here before this one fell.

That was a first, that morning, in his eleventh grade history class. When all of the girls began to wail, when the boys did too, as they watched the buildings burn in New York City. Burn and then fall. That was a first.

He did what he had to do, what he was compelled to do.

Nate signed up.

Four tours as a Ranger, one in Iraq and three in Afghanistan, and this happened before, in a different way, the cries in the dark, in the smoke. There was a first time, in a village, and then it was a past thing.

The inky blackness was something new, a first, was a thing.

He was calm.

The EMP, the tremor, he recognized those, the darkness that fell as a blanket, that brought blindness to himself and everyone on the floor. That was new. The way it soaked him to the bone, a first. A weapon he'd not seen before. Before now. Some nerve agent, perhaps.

He was calm.

This was not the first time he'd sat in the dark. He'd done that before. But not this inky blackness. Not in Afghanistan. The nights in Afghanistan were never this dark. Quite the contrary, on some nights visibility was as high as thirty percent. No, he sat in the dark, in the black, somewhere else. Somewhere that wasn't on a map. A place that a passing ship might mistake for an oil rig, except it wasn't an oil rig. It was a black site, a black site with a tight black box, a dark black box. He sat in there, in the tight box, for two days. They all did at some point. He thought of them, his brothers. He thought of those that were left, those that came home, and he bided the time, kept track of time the way he was trained, kept calm until his vision, until everyone's vision, returned.

Nate calculated a day had passed.

When his vision came back, it was as if someone flicked a switch — dark, and then light. He slid himself out from under the desk where he bunked himself. He was alone in the high-walled cubicle, though he could hear others shuffling about, a woman still crying. The lights in the ceiling panels above were off, but a gray day glow lit the room. He lifted the black plastic receiver from the phone. There were a dozen little white buttons above the number pad and a blank digital screen. He could guess how to access an outside line, but it made no difference, no matter what he tapped, no tone. The phone was dead.

He fished out his smart phone from his new Men's Wearhouse sport coat on the back of the office chair. That too, dead.

There was an EMP over the city, of that he was sure.

He'd rolled his cuffs up to the top of his forearms during the time the lights were out and contemplated now if he wanted anyone to see the mass of Polynesian ink that ran down his left wrist. He decided not, and rolled the sleeves down. Then he tightened his tie and grabbed his jacket, but he didn't put it on.

Nate made his way out of the little maze of high cubicle walls to the main aisle that ran the ring of the office. Private glassed offices and suites lined the outer wall. The one in front of him was empty. A bright mist hung beyond the window.

The next office was occupied. Behind the desk, facing him, was Deidra, the HR woman that had welcomed him to Titan the day before. She was resting her chin on her thumbs. Her elbows were propped up on her desk, the fist of one hand tightly closed in the other, her fingers forming a steeple. The ink of her mascara was smudged in thick raccoon lines around glassy vein-laden eyes that had cried in their blindness. Her yellow curls were loose and away from her scalp, unfurled. And her thousand-mile stare was aimed toward the desktop, sixteen inches away.

"Deidra," Nate said.

She didn't respond.

The tension of the last twenty-four hours — he thought. She might be in shock. "Deidra," he said again, this time leaning through the threshold of the office door. Her eyes rolled up at him. She sniffled and forced a smile.

Nate stepped in, tore a peach tissue from the embroidered cube at the side of her desk and offered it to her. She pinched it between her fingers, peered into his eyes, sniffled again, and then dabbed herself with the paper cloth. The action must've grounded her because she lashed out for two more tissues — *thip, thip* — and made quick work of bringing herself back around.

Nate waited. Deidra needed a purpose. He'd give her one.

She tossed the used tissue into the basket beneath her desk

and with her fingertips spread wide, she pressed her white blouse into place, from her shoulder to her waist, smoothing out the wrinkle that had begun to form near her arms and at her midline. Then she gave Nate her bravest face.

"Nathan Farthen," she said. "Right?"

He made sure to keep his voice leveled, kind, "Nate is fine," he said.

"Yes, yes. Nate." Her pupils darted past him and to the sides of the office.

"We had an event," he said.

"We did." Deidra nodded, concerned.

"The power is out, which means the elevator is most likely out, and we're on the eighty-fifth floor."

"The power is out?"

"Focus, Deidra. Is there a protocol? You're Human Resources, you must know if there's a protocol. What are you supposed to do if there's a power outage? If there's an…" He stopped himself. Those words. *An attack*. Those words wouldn't help the situation, wouldn't put Deidra's head where he needed her to be. The way to control the situation was to keep her calm, to keep everyone calm.

"A power outage?"

"Yes," Nate said, "a power outage."

"We have a protocol."

"Great. I thought so. I mean, you seem very organized. What is it?"

"We stay here."

"Stay here?"

"In the event of a power outage. We stay on the floor until someone notifies us or someone comes."

"So we sit tight? That's it?"

Nate was aware of the finer details of what happened to the last building that occupied this block, what had happened to those that were told to stay on their floors and wait. It was also the right thing to do.

"First we do a head count," Deidra said, "so we can call…" Her eyes shifted to the black phone on her desk. She was already aware it didn't work.

Nate didn't want her to ponder. "A head count. And who does that?"

Deidra's eyes went wide. "I do," she said. "I'm the floor warden." She spun to the side and then rose from her chair. She swung up the door to the compartment overhanging her desk unit and from between a stack of stapled papers and a dried out plant, removed a shiny yellow plastic construction helmet. She plopped it on her head, forcing her curls to sprout out sideways around the rim, and then straightened the front of her skirt as she had her blouse. She opened a cabinet drawer just below the desktop, removed a flashlight and clipboard, and then flicked the switch of the light to check it.

Nate bit his lip when the light didn't go on.

"I just bought batteries," she said. She set the flashlight down and went to work filling out the paper attached to the clipboard line by line.

"Today is the twenty-sec—"

"The twenty-third," Nate corrected.

Deidra's lips went tight across her face. "The twenty-third." The top of the pen bobbed rapidly as she checked two of a series of boxes. "Occupied?" she mumbled. "Obviously... Time?" She looked at the tiny sparkling watch on her wrist. "My watch stopped."

Nate flipped his wrist over. EMP, all right. "Did it stop at 12:23?"

"Yeah, 12:23." Deidra grinned and cocked an eyebrow. "How did you know?"

"I keep exact time," Nate said.

"Me too." She scrawled the time down on the clipboard and then glanced up at Nate. "But how is it your watch stopped at the same time?"

"The outage. It's that kind of outage. Anything electric. That why the phones and the flashlight don't work."

"Oh." Deidra tapped her lower lip with the end of her pen. "Anything electronic?"

"Uh huh."

"Cory," Deidra said under her breath.

Nate realized she was merely speaking out loud and not to him, yet he asked, "Who?"

Without an answer, Deidra stormed past Nate, out of her office and into the aisle. "Cory," she repeated as she walked. Nate followed her. At the end of the aisle a black woman with a beehive hairdo was stretching her arms.

"Iona?" Deidra asked. "Have you seen Cory?"

The woman gazed down the aisle and shook her head.

The cubicles were empty, up until the third. Deidra stopped and threw her hand flat up against her nose. Nate caught the odor when he neared. Cory, a husky twenty-something man, was slumped down in his Aeron chair. He'd defecated himself when he died.

"He had a pacemaker," Deidre said, "an electric one. He joked that if the power ever went out he would…" She wobbled her head to the side. "He's been right there, all night."

Deidra lifted her clipboard and began jotting down the details of Cory's demise.

Nate looked past her shoulder to Iona, who was now rolling her neck in a circle.

He decided he wanted to get a lay of the land.

"I'll be right back," he said.

"Okay."

Nate stopped two steps away and then pivoted back around.

"Who else should be here?" he asked.

"Most everybody goes to lunch. Jenny, Henry's assistant, she'll be here for sure. Maybe the marketing team on the far side."

Nate nodded and headed out on his mission to survey the floor. He smiled at Iona and she smiled back, but he gave her space as he rounded the corner.

The floor was essentially a square with the elevators, stairwell, and core in the center. Nate saw the girl he thought must be Jenny sitting at the end of the aisle. She was a Native American, or Polynesian, Nate wasn't sure. She was a big girl, heavyset, with full round cheeks, and a sad smile. A pleasant smile, but sad just the same. That was understandable. He didn't expect to find anyone happy, or dancing. The cubicles on this side were two deep and the walls lower than where he'd been seated, chest high, but he didn't see anyone standing in them. The glassed offices on this side were nicer, darker finished woods; they would've overlooked the financial district, but a fog blocked any view. The limited light, along with the dark walnut hues, gave the offices a heavy shadow. Midway across the floor he saw a silhouette. Nate stopped and peered through the glass wall. A portly man in a sport coat and tie was writing on a legal pad. He lifted his porcine head to look back at Nate.

"Are you from downstairs?" the man asked.

"No," Nate said. "Are you all right?"

The man didn't answer.

"Sir?"

"You're not from downstairs?"

Nate shook his head. "No, sir."

The man grunted, waved him away, and then buried his forehead in his hand. Nate watched him for a moment more and then continued toward the girl at the desk.

"You're Jenny?" he asked.

"Yes."

"Are you okay?"

Jenny nodded her head.

"Is there anyone else over here?"

She tilted her head to the office to her right. Nate leaned forward to see in. The office was three times the size of the others that he'd passed, a large suite, Henry's office. Henry, a tall man in a pressed white shirt and tight-fitting olive green slacks, was standing arms akimbo at his windowed wall, staring out into the abyss.

"Do you mind?" Nate asked Jenny.

She shrugged.

He circled her desk to the office and rattled his knuckles on Henry's doorframe.

The man across the office answered with a Brit accent. "How can I help you?"

"Excuse me," Nate said. "I was just —"

Henry spun to face him. "Come in. Come in."

Nate nodded and entered the room.

"Hi," Nate said. "I'm —"

Henry cut him off again. "Nathan Farthen." Henry held up a hand to greet him. "The Ranger. I know who everyone is coming into this office."

"Of course. Nate is fine."

Henry took Nate's hand firmly into his own. His smile was reassuring and apart from a slight shadow of a beard, he appeared to be in prime form. "Sit down," he said, gesturing to the leather couch on the side of the suite.

Nate lifted both of his hands. "Thank you, but..."

"Right," Henry said. "Me too."

Henry walked back over to the glass and resumed glaring into the fog.

"EMP, you think?"

"Yeah," Nate said. "Something twenty-five, thirty klicks up."

"And the tremor?"

"It must have been large. Megaton."

Henry nodded in thought. Then he added. "I was concerned about the fog," he said, twirling his fingers up and around, "but this building is wired with sensors and Geigers, they'd be going berserk if there was any fallout or radioactive residue."

"Except for the EMP."

Henry shrugged, widened his eyes, and nodded. "Except for the EMP. There is that, could've knocked the sensors out."

"I'm sure of it."

Henry continued to stare into the mist.

"I wouldn't worry about contamination though," Nate added.

Henry veered back toward him. "No?"

"Doesn't work that way... If it was even a nuke."

"Right." The smile returned. "What's next, do you suppose?"

"Hold tight."

Deidra tapped on the doorframe. Iona was behind her as well as a skinny young Indian man in khakis and a polo shirt. "Henry," she said.

"Yes, Deidra?"

"Cory is dead."

Henry gave Nate a side glance before addressing her. "His pacemaker," he said. "And the others? How many others are on the floor?"

Nate noted Henry didn't mention the past twenty-four hours, not the EMP, not the prolonged darkness that followed, not the black raccoon circles surrounding Deidra's eyes. He was a leader going forward.

Deidra lifted her clipboard and pen and began to list the names. "There are ten of us altogether. Mister Farther, myself, Cory, deceased, Iona, Bruce — he's in his office — Raj, Jenny, Lisa, Terry, and Rob, back in Marketing, and you. Everyone else appears to be off the floor."

"Ten souls," Henry said, his words seemed to drift with some second intent, some memory. Nate wondered if Henry too was a veteran of some war, some other place. "Well, why don't you round everybody up? We'll move into the conference room for lunch. If anyone has anything left from yesterday, they should bring it. I believe we have crisps and such in the break room and I'll spring for the soda machine. We'll sit tight, and help will be along soon."

~*~

~3~

Without the rumble of elevator bay, the hum of the computers, desk fans, heating and cooling units, or any other electrical device on the high floor, the smallest of sounds became amplified. A bubble surging to the surface of the water cooler was thunderous, the carbonation release from an uncapped seltzer could be heard in every corner of the office. Without the forced air circulation the same was true for smell. The aroma of potato chips and pretzels, long since devoured, lingered in the foil bags they were packaged in. After a few short days on the floor, the odors of their own clothes were inescapable. Nate's new Men's Wearhouse khakis reeked of the sweet scent of sweat, a smell he could no longer ignore.

They'd all done their best to stay fresh. The women dabbed cologne. Ironically, Jenny and Iona appeared no different than they had the day before. Jenny, preferring her own desk, went back there in the morning to knit. It could've been another normal day. Lisa and Terry, the young women from Marketing, were dressed for after-work cocktail hour, so they merely appeared to have stayed out late and not made it home before coming in to the office. Poor Deidra showed the brunt of forty-eight hours on the floor. Her attempts to clean away the raccoon mascara left ten years on her face that weren't there before. She did her best to busy herself until it was too dark to work, yet Nate heard her whimpers deep into the night.

The others pretended not to notice.

What couldn't be ignored was the need for food. They'd cleared the snacks from the pantry and had now gone a day without eating.

They were expecting the cavalry at any time, but no one came before nightfall, and as midday rolled around relief was still nowhere in sight.

Nate was up for food, but he wasn't hungry, not much. Bruce, on the other hand, was in the midst of some 'sugar situation.' That's what Iona called it when he wandered off. "He's got the 'sugar,' " she said.

Nate was familiar with the term. His grandmother said 'the sugar' when she spoke of diabetes. Grandpa had 'the sugar' too. And it was a safe bet that Bruce, five-nine, age fifty, and two hundred and thirty or so pounds had Type Two, a real safe bet. Where the others were either disregarding or in distress of their situation, Bruce was angry, frustrated, and more focused on the time creep the incident would put on his project. Nate's impression was that Bruce was an ass, though the others appeared unfazed by his demeanor — to them Bruce was just being Bruce. Some agreed with his reasoning when he argued that they should head to the cafeteria, one flight above.

"This is ridiculous," he said. "There's a ton of food just over our heads."

"He's got a point," Rob said. Rob was the Marketing VP and even without corporate experience, Nate was able to size him up. He'd met a dozen Robs before, either in the form of a salesman or lawyer, oily con men that never seemed to commit to one side or the other, always working their own agenda a thin layer behind those *trust me* eyes. And Rob had the works. Nate supposed that was the difference between sales and marketing, between a five-digit and a six-digit payroll. Rob's slacks and monogrammed shirt certainly weren't from Men's Wearhouse, and there was enough product in his hair and Van Dyke beard to keep him quaffed for a week, less the two days they'd already spent on the floor. "How about," Rob said, "Bruce and I run upstairs, see what we can find. And then we bring it back down here. That way if anyone comes along, you'll be waiting."

Henry nodded and Nate didn't bother to answer.

"I'll help," Terry, one of Rob's Marketeers, added. From the little black cocktail dress she was wearing and the way she kept her gaze on Rob, Nate assumed her job was to stick close to him.

Everyone agreed, and nothing more was said until after they left the floor through Marketing. The hair on his neck rose and he thought he perceived a slight pressure change as he watched the fire door to the stairwell open.

That's when Iona began to talk about Bruce and 'the sugar.' Nate lifted himself out of the pleather-cushioned chair, his seat for the past hour, and moved over to the glass wall. Henry was staring out again, Bruce's moment of distraction having passed, but he gave the man space.

There wasn't anything new to see out in the creamy fog, and there wasn't too much to be said.

But Nate didn't stand there long.

From above their heads came a crash, a loud smash that on the all-too-silent floor mimicked thunder, and outside of the window, though he couldn't be sure, Nate saw several shards of glass. He was not sure, because they didn't drop, they didn't fall, rather they held just beyond clarity in the mist, allowing only brief glints.

He would've examined them more, except he was forced to look up, look up at the source of the severe set of thumps that followed the crash. The foam and plastic ceiling tiles that shielded the now dark lights bounced in their frames with each solid thud, as if a huge hammer was pounding the floor above.

THUMP, THUMP.

"What's happening?" Deidra asked, already showing signs of an understandable panic.

THUMP, THUMP.

"Gas line," Henry said. His head pivoted to Nate for a confirmation to his guess.

THUMP, THUMP.

"Yeah," Nate said. "Something's under pressure.

Something on the end of a line." He said it, but he wasn't sure. It made sense. "The group may've jarred something."

THUMP, THUMP.

Deidra eased up. "Jarred something?" she asked.

THUMP, THUMP.

Henry and Nate simultaneously met eyes. "A fire," Henry said, and began to move toward the door.

"Where's the extinguisher?" Nate asked.

"By the door," Henry said. "Raj, you come with us. Lisa," he said, quickly scanning the other women, "you stay down here."

"A fire?" Iona asked.

"A flash fire," Nate said. "Probably happened when they opened the door, blew out the wall."

"Listen," Raj said.

The men froze.

"It's stopped," he added.

"That may be a good thing," Nate said, and continued out of the lounge.

Then, without warning, came the screams. Nate had heard many screams, too many to count. He only counted the firsts. Horrid pleas, heinous situations, but these were different. These were a first.

Then the shrieks shifted to the conference room and Nate spun back to see who was breaking down. Deidra had her hand flat against the side of her head. Lisa and Iona were already on her, trying to calm her down. Whether the cavalry came in five minutes or five hours, Deidra was never going to be the same.

Raj's jaw was agape.

"Let's go," Nate said.

Henry was already near the door, freeing the huge red canister from the fire bay. He handed Raj the axe. To his right Nate saw the huge guillotine paper cutter the Marketeers used to cut mailings and material. He levered up the two-foot blade, put his right shoe on the wooden base, and with a heave, pried it free. Then he turned to join the other two men at the stairwell door.

He squeezed his grip onto the handle of his new machete-like blade. Henry gave him a slight nod. It hadn't occurred to Nate until then that he was destroying company property, but in the moment, they were beyond such norms, and beyond was a place Nate was comfortable with.

They were met with a hanging mist of white creamy haze.

"There's no smell to this smoke," Raj said as the made their way up the stairwell.

"This isn't smoke. It's the vapor coming down from somewhere," Henry said. "Try not to breath it in, there's a fire door up above."

"Right," Raj said. "Will there be a blaze on the other side?"

"Most likely not," Nate said. "The sprinklers should've done their job."

"Without power?"

"They don't need power. They work off heat."

Henry stopped outside of the door, one hand hovering in front of it, and the other holding the extinguisher.

"So if the fire's out," Raj said, "why do we need all of this?"

"Pockets," Nate said. "The sprinklers can't reach everywhere."

"The door is cool," Henry said. He slipped his free hand down to the handle. "That's cool too."

"Does that mean we can go in?" Raj asked.

Henry peered past Raj to Nate. Nate shrugged.

Henry reached and began to turn the handle.

"The screaming's stopped," Raj said.

Henry glanced at Raj and then proceeded to open the door.

"What the…" Raj said. His arms went limp beside him, the axe hung low. The raw odor of feces and the rancid mix of other inner body juices overwhelmed Raj and he lurched forward to empty his stomach. Since there was nothing there, he merely gagged hard, and then gagged again.

Neither Nate nor Henry said anything. Henry let the extinguisher fall to the floor. There hadn't been a fire. Nothing was burned. The place was in disarray, but there wasn't the slightest sign of char. Nate could see that the far wall was different than the floor below. The glass wasn't shattered. The walls on this level were receded. A wrap-around sky-high patio was the ceiling to the conference room below. The double doors to the patio were slid wide open to the cream fog outside, and between them, a section of the cafeteria.

There were no signs of Rob or Bruce. No Terry in her little black dress.

No signs except for the thinly spread, shining layer of blood and intestinal tract that was pasted across the floor, the walls, the plants, and the scattered remnants of broken chairs and tables. The section of room outside the stairwell door could've been the inside of a mammoth food processor left on too long. Nate had seen people blown apart, vaporized; this was not that. This was a bludgeoning. This was something ground up, chewed up, and spit back out.

Small chunks of reddish brown flesh — parts of the body Nate couldn't readily identify — plopped from the ceiling to the floor and landed with the squish of freshly chopped meat.

Raj, hands on his knees, was taking deep breaths. Nate was breathing through his mouth.

"What do you think...?" Henry began to ask.

"I dunno," Nate said. "An explosion of some kind." He took a step back. "I've never seen a concussion that could—"

"Why did the screams come afterward?" Raj asked. Nate and Henry both looked at the back of the man's head, still bent forward.

The question was a legitimate one. *Why did the screams come afterward?* Nate thought to himself. He gazed out toward the void of the fog. The mist, a wall of white still near the outside of the conference room window below, began to creep across the patio. Nate gave Raj's upper arm a jab with his elbow. Again, the three said nothing. They stared at the blanket of mist slowly moving toward them, eagerly covering the floor as it went. It was through the doors and halfway across the cafeteria before they saw them, the willowy bright wriggling three-foot-long tips of the tentacle arms. One, then three, and then seven, spread across the width of the foot-high rolling fog, twirling and feeling their way forward, forward…

"We have to go," Nate said, and he reached for the handle behind him. With the same grip, he spun himself around, pushed the door open, and pulled himself into the stairwell. Raj and Henry were stuck to his back in their retreat and, rather than burst down the stairs, pushed their weight against the door to ensure it was secure.

And then the three descended the misting stairwell.

"We have to get out of this building," Nate said, squeezing his new two-foot heavy steel with a greater purpose than the trip up.

"Let's get the others and go," Henry said.

Nate didn't bother to ask the other two what they thought they saw, and they didn't ask him. Raj, he figured, was most likely in a state of shock, and Henry and he weren't going to dwell on something they couldn't explain. Things don't come out of the fog, and if they do, they don't come out of the sky on the eighty-sixth floor.

Having been the first back into the stairwell Nate was the first to the Titan floor door. He pulled the handle open without hesitation, took two steps in, and froze. He felt the wood of Raj's axe handle press into his back as Raj ran into him, taken by the same shock.

The door Nate opened didn't open to the eighty-fifth floor, not to the Marketing department, or the conference room on the other side, or to the waiting Iona, Deidra, or Lisa. The door opened to the blood-stained cafeteria and the cluster of tentacles meticulously inspecting the center of the room.

"This can't be," Raj said.

Nate pushed him back and then pivoted to get through the door. "Go, go, go."

They scurried down the misty stairs again, this time Henry leading the way, and when they reached the next flight, he peeked in and gave the other two a reassuring nod before fully opening the door.

Why did the screams come afterward? Nate thought again. Now it made sense, except it didn't make sense. They — Rob and

Terry and Bruce — had probably run to escape the cafeteria and had landed back into the trap. It made sense but it didn't make sense.

This time they weren't on the floor of the cafeteria, but they weren't on the eighty-fifth floor either. The glass walls were sloped up to the open floor above and to the floor below, three flights combined, their levels intermingled.

"Where are we?" Nate asked. "This can't be the eighty-fourth floor."

"No," Henry said. "A hundred and first. We're on the observation level."

"No escape," Raj said.

"What's that?" Nate asked.

"We're in Naraka."

"Naraka?"

"Naraka is Hindi, it's like the western purgatory, or hell. There is no escape. Our souls were sent here to make amends for our sins."

"You don't seriously believe in that?" Nate asked.

"Look." Raj gestured over the railing to the rolling mist on the level below. The mist filled an alcove in a swirl and then dissipated, leaving in its place the blurred figure of a person, of a man or a woman, Nate couldn't be sure. The near transparent figure appeared to wrestle with its surroundings, as if the air around it was crushing the creature. A muffled faraway scream echoed off the high-sloped glass from no particular direction, and the misting fog enveloped the shadow of a being as both faded to nothing.

"You see?" Raj said. "You don't have to believe."

~*~

~4~

The stairwell was different than the day before, the mist no longer a floating vapor, rather a hanging cloud. They didn't have to travel far, one floor at a time was suffice to end up anywhere, and it didn't seem to matter if they ascended or descended because the floor the door opened up to would be the luck of the draw. They went as high as the observation deck and as low as the forty-third, twenty stories at a time, never traveling more than a flight between doors. Nate and Henry were the only ones focused on their search for... well, first for a way out, and then for food, and then just searching. Nate thought he heard some people behind the doors more than once, but the floors were always empty, of people anyway. Of living people.

They didn't return to the cafeteria, or to the Titan offices on the eighty-fifth floor. They came across the tentacles again though, in other places, and other things, glimmers, things they didn't stick around to investigate. Some of the floors, where the glass walls had shattered and the mist was fuller, were too unsettling to step through. Objects hung midair, suspended for no reason, not flying, not falling, simply arrested in place — a phone, trash bins, a family photo from someone's desk hanging in an aisle, the glass punched out of the frame, all floating. And those floors — maybe due to the air, the altitude, or the pressure — were a physical struggle of vertigo and nausea.

Raj was an incessantly chatting shadow. Repeating nonsense about Naraka and purgatory and hell and demons and apologies — Nate tuned him out and moved him along.

They found a jackpot of food on a floor where the word Wonderco was painted in red across a yellow wall by the elevator, a dot-com, Nate figured, because the entire place was painted in festival colors. There were beanbags and air cushions, and a huge pantry with a dry cereal and fruit buffet where huge plastic containers of rainbow-colored Fruity Pebbles, granola, cornflakes, and M&Ms hung in a row, beside bowls of bananas, apples, and oranges. Only a few days old, the fruit was a bounty, as was the refrigerator full of Parmalat. The fridge was out but the small cartons of long life milk didn't need refrigeration to stay fresh. In the cupboards below, Nate found five plastic wrapped yellow backpacks with the Wonderco logo printed across the top. He pulled them out, tossed them on the counter. The three feasted on the milk and fruit and cornflakes while Henry and Nate stuffed the packs with what food they could carry.

When they were done they rested on the beanbags.

Raj began to snore as soon as his head was down.

"It's the stress," Henry said.

"You don't really think he's coming back?" Nate asked.

"Oh, no. I just meant that the stress wore on him quickly."

"And you?"

Henry pursed his lips and Nate couldn't help but think that rather than spitting out the truth, the man was sizing up an answer to fit the situation. "I think I see what you're getting at. Who in their right mind wouldn't be stressed? Stress can't be avoided, but I don't think that we, the two of us, are that different in terms of stress."

Nate scooted down and back into the huge beanbag pillow. He grinned at Henry and then said, "I just wanted to start my new job."

"I'm sure you did. But that's what I mean. The stress is a tool, a vehicle to go forward," Henry glanced at Raj, snorting air in through his nose, "not a place to check out."

"Checking out isn't all that bad. I mean, if you can't go back. He's never seen anything..." Nate caught himself. He didn't want to share too much. Not that he saw that as an issue with Henry, he just didn't want to go there, to that place. "I'll be glad to get out of here."

"I agree," Henry said. "I'm glad we found food. I'll feel better when we get some to the others, and best when we get out of here."

~*~

~5~

Not once in the next week did Nate return to the eighty-fifth floor. He, Henry, and Raj did stumble into the cafeteria on eighty-six three more times, but that was as close as they ever got to returning to the coworkers they'd left behind. When they came across the cafeteria they took what they could carry and moved on; it didn't matter if it was a 'blood floor.' By this time they'd found that there were a lot of blood floors.

More and more the stairwell doors opened to floors that were missing outer walls, entire panes of the thick glass torn from the building's side. There were more floors where the rules of physics didn't apply, where objects hung midair, as did the sounds of doors opening, slamming shut, of laughter, and screams, the origins of all unfound. Nate discovered these odd floors — too unsettling to enter in the first days — were good for water, because for whatever reason the faucets in the bathrooms still worked, the toilets still flushed. He became so quickly accustomed to the weird physics that he would set his things next to him in midair without even thinking about it. He'd set his razor on an invisible counter while he shaved, let his paper cutter sword suspend while he went through the drawers of a desk. He became so used to the lack of 'normal' that when he was on a normal floor he would forget himself and do the same, only to find his blade or other object let loose and fall to the floor.

They weren't moving floor to floor as rapidly as they did

the first few days. There wasn't much point in rushing, and not every floor had food. There was a day when every door opened to mirrored sets of cubicles, row upon row of empty workspaces, and nothing else. They spent an entire day without food and water. They almost lost Raj that day, so their habits changed. If they found a floor with a pantry or any food at all, they stayed for a while.

Raj listened and did what he was told, but no longer conversed, merely mumbled to himself, more so when he was upset. Henry was good for conversation, if there was anything to talk about, but there usually wasn't. There hadn't been anything new to discuss for days, days delineated by the shades of gray gleam emitting from the shrouding creamy mist.

Hunger wasn't the greatest risk. There were other things they'd encountered that were far worse. There were the upper floors — that they could walk into from below — with the little bubbles of shifting reality. There was the hive floor. Spooked from a floor, they traversed the stairwell in the dark, opened a door, and were attacked by a swarm, a flock of flying blue eels. Henry, the last off the floor, took the brunt of the attack, his yellow Wonderco shoulder pack was near shredded as he squeezed out the door. Of these though, the tentacle creatures hiding, prowling in the mist were the greater risk of all. Any open windowed floor meant the potential wriggle then lash. And they weren't all little arms like those they first saw on eighty-six. There were greater creatures out there, creatures with pipes for limbs, creatures that could smash a man to paste and then spread him jam and butter onto every surface of a room. They'd seen the remains on the blood floors and had near encounters more than once. Had seen the long arms probing through the length of a room when they peeked inside. The creatures were a constant danger. Nate, Henry, and Raj moved slowly between floors. They were prey.

And they were on the move again, wary of whatever may be on the prowl.

They were on one of the odd floors. There was cereal again — not in bins though — in little boxes with cartoon characters on the front. The milk cartons in the glass door cooler were foul, but they'd stretched the Parmalat and had plenty left. The next time he came across Parmalat, that was all Nate planned to carry. He was leaning back against the counter, a bowl of milk-covered Raisin Bran in his hand, his jaw machine grinding each bite. He was watching Raj.

Raj was sitting at one of the two small café tables to the side of the pantry, twirling an apple from one hand to another with the tips of his fingers, a waxed apple that appeared as if it could've been plucked from the orchard that morning. Raj was mumbling almost to an audible level, but it was what Nate deemed a happy mumble. He wondered if Raj saw an apple or a ball. He'd wait a moment and then tell him to eat. Raj moved better if he ate. Henry was rifling through the pantry's top cupboards. Nate was used to this too, Henry's search for something more than there was to offer.

"I'll be," Henry said.

Nate's eyes rolled far right to see what Henry had discovered. It was a forest green cube tin. "What you have there?" Nate asked, though he was already aware of what was inside. One of his buddies had a tin like that, though he stored a different loose leaf inside.

"This," Henry said, holding the tin high, "you cannot get stateside." Nate noticed the tin was still plastic sealed. "Somebody brought this treasure here, special."

"Well, there ya go," Nate said. "It's yours now."

Henry gave the tin a closer inspection. "It's mine now," he agreed.

"How you going to heat it?"

"We'll find a way. It won't go to waste, I assure you. In fact, I think I may have a cup now." He knelt down and opened a lower cupboard door. "And bingo." He slid a full case of Sterno from the middle shelf. Nate tried to recall a smile on Henry's face before this one. Another first.

A crash from the outer office stole the smile from Henry. Something heavy met the floor, a phone, or perhaps a monitor. Nate froze, the plastic spoon pinched snug between his thumb and fingers, hanging three inches from his mouth. He didn't breathe. Another crash, definitely something flung from a desk.

Nate maneuvered the paper cereal bowl around to the counter and swapped it for his paper cutter machete.

Raj stared at Nate in wait for instructions to flee. He no longer twirled the apple. His fingertips pressed into the table; his hands were claws.

Henry gently, quietly, pressed the Sterno back into the cupboard.

Nate pressed a hand forward toward Raj, and then nodded to Henry, one gesture to remain, the other to follow. Henry held a butcher knife he'd retrieved from another office pantry. Not much of an arsenal, but Nate's plan wasn't to fight. He just wanted to see what was out there, because if one of those tentacle creatures loomed nearby he and Henry were going the other way.

The pantry was in the midst of a work area, two partitions and a café centrally located. The racket traveled from the other side of the partition, toward the corner. That was good. Nate wanted a peek, and if there was trouble, he'd grab Raj and head toward the stairwell door in the other direction.

He walked lightly yet held his blade high, ready to swing heavy. He approached the end of the pantry, prepared to round the corner, and then leaned forward, the cutter high behind his ear.

Another crash.

Nate froze.

He sucked a silent breath through his nose, and let his weight rest on his forward left foot. He leaned further in.

He expected to see the wavering mist, the fog, coursing across the carpeted floor, over the work tables, exploring, and from the thick creamy cotton haze a tentacle, probing, prowling.

But when Nate leaned forward that's not what he found.

There was no mist stealing in from the corner of the floor, no break in the outer wall they'd missed, no tentacle exploring the surface of the tables.

There was something else.

There was someone else, a woman in a black dress. She was straightening the fabric, stretching the hem of the material down, and then she began to rake her fingers through her hair.

Slowly he lowered the cutter to his side and rolled his head around his neck, in awe of the stranger. Henry joined him by his side, and he too stilled upon seeing the woman.

"Terry?" Henry asked. But the Marketeer in the cocktail dress said nothing.

~*~

~6~

Nate had spent a day with Terry. That was all, one day, a lifetime ago. But once Henry mentioned her name, he recognized the young woman — her hourglass body, jet-black hair up in a bun before, now fallen to her shoulders. Her arms floated away from her hair and face, as if she was unaware of their presence. She didn't set eyes on them. Nate was deciding if she was catatonic, as Raj had become. It was possible she'd been alone since leaving the eighty-fifth floor. Or maybe this was a ruse and she was aiming to flee.

She may've been ignoring them altogether, unsure if they were even real.

A rattle to Nate's right caused her to stiffen.

He swung his head in time to see a pencil cup fall to the carpeted floor and gently roll to a stop.

She wasn't ignoring them. There was something else on the floor, hidden from where Nate stood.

Nate's eyes darted to either side of the room and then he slowly cranked his neck to peek toward the stairwell.

Slinking over the plain table desks was a single probing tentacle. He marveled at how long the arm must be, extending forty feet at least, yet only the fine tip explored the surface of the table, delicately swiveling around the lamp, the phone, sliding an abandoned legal pad to the edge and onto the floor with the cup.

The tentacle reached back to the exits, yet he saw no trace

of mist to detail exactly from where the creature was entering. They could possibly go to the wall. This was an open floor with no outer suites and on arrival they'd found no glass disturbed – but that may've changed. Maybe they could wait it out, keep moving around the edges, outmaneuver the probing arm and make their exit in a loop. But there may be another and they would succumb to a trap.

A flush of heat filled Nate as his blood began to pump adrenalin.

He glanced at Henry. The Brit gave a nod down the aisle toward the stairwell, and Nate was glad for it. Best to scope the way out first. He repeated his gestures to Raj and Henry — remain and follow — and then he began to heel-toe forward, his cutter raised high in his leading right hand, poised to strike.

With a few short steps he was parallel to the tip of the creature.

Nate gave a hard look at the rows of tiny serrated suction cups lining the bottom half of the wriggling limb. The blood red tentacle appeared not to notice him.

He glanced back at Terry. She was watching his progression. The light behind her eyes let him know she was still very much there. He gave her a soft smile and she responded in kind. On that sole day they spent in the conference room she'd only had a stern look on her face. Annoyed her phone wasn't working, that her plans were disturbed, that she was forced into the company of the others. The face she wore now was of a changed woman. Nate peeked to the tentacle, back to her, and signaled with his free hand for her to come. He sent the same signal to Raj and then raised his index finger to his mouth.

Henry stopped so that Terry and Raj could slip into line while Nate led the way.

And the way was slow. The four continued to the exit, Nate, Terry, Raj, and Henry silently hugging the shadowed wall as they went. Breathing as lightly as possible, taking gentle steps as the red writhing rope width of monster flesh running beside them continued to slither further into the room.

When Nate reached the edge of the interior wall, he saw the entry point of the invading beast. The incredibly lengthy probe stemmed from a misty floor vent.

He stopped and peeked around the wall to see if there were any other uninvited guests waiting for them. There weren't. Their way to the door was clear.

Nate turned back to the three, tilted his head to the entrance, and mouthed, "Let's go."

His head wasn't fully back forward when, from the corner of his eye, he saw Raj drop his shiny waxed apple. Nate's face must've been telltale because he saw his horror reflected in Terry's. She spun in time for both to see Henry's fingers lunging, clutching for Raj's pack as the out of sorts man bent toward the desk for the rolling apple.

And then Raj bumped the desk.

The response of the tentacle was immediate.

Henry spun left and dropped down to avoid the recoil of the three meters of whip bearing toward him, the butcher knife blocking his face.

Raj was too late to react. By the time he screamed he was thrashed above Nate and Terry and slammed in between the ceiling above and desks below. The scream ceased on impact.

In the instant the beast had sprung to life Nate had pushed his back into the wall. What had been Raj was a pasted jelly. Nate's eyes darted the length of the tentacle. The root of the arm near the vent undulated in a short arc. If he acted, he could get close. If he didn't, they were next.

With one liquid motion he launched himself from the end of the wall and thrust his paper cutter blade down through the crimson flesh of the beast.

A thunderous shriek echoed up through the floor as both ends of cut tentacle began to spout fountains of blood.

The tentacle was cut but there were four meters of length to the vent. Nate began hacking wildly, working to move closer to the source.

From the vent the tip of another tentacle began to creep through. Nate wanted to get closer but his fight with the wounded limb kept him at bay.

Then to his left flew a chair, and then another. He looked over to see Terry franticly throwing whatever furniture she could lift. They were on the offensive.

Invigorated, he swung the blade down harder, hitting his mark and hacking two feet off at a time, making his way toward the second tentacle.

Then he saw Henry.

Using a flat panel monitor as a shield, he rolled up to the vent and with one slash, severed the two limbs clean at the grate.

Nate rushed over to help Henry flip a table upside down on the vent. Then they slid the nearby copy machine to the table and pushed the heavy box on its side.

His arms, shirt, and Men's Wearhouse khakis were coated in blood. And so were Henry's. Terry somehow escaped the worst of the fount.

"What now?" Terry asked.

"Well," Nate said, "we'll find a floor with running water. Clean up."

She nodded and brought the back of her hand across the bridge of her nose. "That'll be good."

"First though, I think we should eat. I haven't had meat in weeks."

Henry grinned. "I'll get the Sterno."

~*~

~7~

It took another week to find a floor with running water. It was, of course, one of the floors where physics didn't matter. The floor had an executive gym, which meant showers, and showers with enough force to propel water down, so even with objects floating and suspended the three of them reveled in properly cleaning themselves and their clothes.

Nate finished and dressed before the others. The changing area reminded him of places he'd only seen in movies. The lockers were hardwood, not metal, and mosaic tile covered the walls. It was a comforting place and he decided he'd rather wait there than out on the odd floor. He sat at the end of the dark lacquered wooden bench with his back to the wall, one arm on his knees, one hand playing with a suspending piece of glass, twirling the jagged shard midair. On a bench next to him was a Sony Walkman, not an iPod or an mp3 player or even a Discman, but an old Walkman, plugged into a wall charger. He grinned and picked up the old tape player to examine it, but the cord wasn't long enough to pull over so he reached to unplug it. That's when he saw that the green light of the charger was on.

He looked up at the nonfunctioning lights and began to question how the outlet could work and then remembered that objects floated here. This was an odd floor.

He slid the old headphones onto his head and hit the eject button to spy the cassette — a no brand mixed tape. He slapped the tape back in, pushed play, and watched it through the small plastic window. The tape began to turn on its spindle. At first there was only the fizzy sound of static and he thought the antique was a piece a junk. Then, with a breath of new life, the ostinato of Zeppelin's Kashmir burst into his brain. A grin crept across his face as he stood and clipped the silver plastic box to his waist. With a swagger, he set out to patrol the echoing halls of suspended glass, rolling his shoulders to the beat, the two-foot paper cutter blade tapping the side of his leg as he walked.

As he exited the gym a thirty-foot tentacle struck out of the mist with lighting ferocity.

Instinctively, so did he.

~*~

ABOUT THE AUTHOR

Daniel Arthur Smith is the author of the international bestsellers **HUGH HOWEY LIVES, THE CATHARI TREASURE, THE SOMALI DECEPTION**, and a few other novels and short stories.

He was raised in Michigan and graduated from Western Michigan University where he studied philosophy, with focus on cognitive science, meta-physics, and comparative religion.

He began his career as a bartender, barista, poetry house proprietor, teacher, and then became a technologist and futurist for the Fortune 100 across the Americas and Europe.

Daniel has traveled to over 300 cities in 22 countries, residing in Los Angeles, Kalamazoo, Prague, Crete, and now writes in Manhattan where he lives with his wife and young sons.

For more information, visit danielarthursmith.com

~*~